THE CASTLE ON HESTER STREET

•

LINDA HELLER

The Jewish Publication Society of America   •   Philadelphia   5742 / 1982

For my grandparents who came to America
and for my parents who told me about them

Text and illustrations copyright © 1982 by Linda Heller
All rights reserved   First edition   Manufactured in the United States of America
Designed by Adrianne Onderdonk Dudden
Library of Congress Cataloging in Publication Data
Heller, Linda.
The castle on Hester Street.
Summary: Julie's grandmother deflates many of her husband's tall tales
about their journey from Russia to America and their life on Hester Street.
[1. Jews — United States — Fiction. 2. Humorous stories] I. Title.
PZ7.H37424Cas   [E]   82-136
ISBN 0-8276-0206-5   AACR2

One day while Julie was visiting her grandparents, her grandfather said, "Did I ever tell you about my good friend Moishe?"

"You told me about Hershel, the famous astronomer," Julie said with a giggle, "the one who discovered that the moon is a matzah ball.

"And you told me about Bessie, your little cousin whose braids were so long she used them for jump ropes. But you never told me about Moishe."

"Moishe the goat was from my village in Russia," Julie's grandfather said. "He pulled the wagon I rode in when I came to America. Not only could Moishe leap across oceans the way others jump over puddles, but he also could sing. We started singing the moment we left Russia. '9,092 miles to go, 9,092 miles, after we pass that small patch of snow we'll have 9,091 miles to go.'"

Julie was about to join in, when her grandmother said, "Sol, what are you telling that child?"

"A true story, just the way I remember it, Rose dear," Julie's grandfather said. "Moishe's wagon was solid gold. It shone like a shooting star when we flew over the ocean."

"That's a story all right, but it's not true!" Julie's grandmother said.

"Grandpa came on a boat, like I did. It was terrible. Hundreds of families were crowded together. Babies were crying. Bundles were piled all over. The boat rocked so much I thought we would drown. But in Russia, life for Jews was very hard. We couldn't live or work where we wanted. Sometimes we were attacked just because we were Jews. We had to leave Russia any way we could."

As her grandmother spoke, pictures grew in Julie's mind of her grandparents leaving their country and crossing a rough winter ocean on a boat so crowded they could hardly move.

"Grandpa, is that how you really came?" Julie asked, looking sad.

"Yes, it was," Julie's grandfather said. He, too, looked sad, until he added, "But what a welcome I got when I arrived. President Theodore Roosevelt rode his horse through a blizzard of ticker tape to greet me. 'Hello, Sol,' he said. 'Mighty glad you could come.'"

"Don't listen to another word," Julie's grandmother said. "Grandpa's brother Morris met him. The boat docked first at Ellis Island. We sat for hours and waited to be inspected. Not everyone who came could stay. If you were sick, you had to go back. I was so afraid they would find something wrong with me, but, thank God, I passed every test."

"Hooray!" Julie shouted.

"Thank you, dear," Julie's grandmother said. She gave her a kiss and said, "I have something to show you." Then she went to the closet.

Julie's grandfather leaned closer and whispered to Julie, "Everyone who came here was given a castle. Mine was on Hester Street. It was so tall the pigeons couldn't fly all the way up to the roof. I had to carry them there."

Julie's grandmother came back to the sofa carrying a box. "Did grandpa tell you about the horrible little room he shared with Louie, the cigarmaker, and Herman, the tailor?" she asked as she sat down. "In those days people had to take in boarders to help pay the rent. Life was hard. Grandpa had a pushcart. He sold buttons fourteen hours a day, six days a week. The only rest he got was on the Sabbath."

"Poor grandpa," Julie said and she patted his hand.

Julie's grandfather was quiet for a moment, then he said, "But what buttons I had! Buttons carved from diamonds, emeralds, and rubies. Buttons big as saucers. Buttons big as plates. Buttons you could use as sleds in the snow."

Julie's grandmother sighed loudly. "Grandpa sold small buttons, small enough to fit through buttonholes. I'll show you," she said as she opened the box. The box was filled with photographs. Julie's grandmother took out an old photograph in a cardboard frame. In it Julie's grandfather stood next to his pushcart, which was full of little buttons.

"Grandpa looks so strong," Julie said, feeling proud.

Julie's grandfather found a photograph of a young girl and showed it to Julie.

"This is a picture of your grandmother," he said. "She was very famous in those days."

"Everyone spoke of Mr. Witkin's beautiful daughter Rose, who stayed home all day nibbling chocolates. Her five big brothers had to watch so that nobody stole her away."

"I worked six days a week in a factory then, sewing dresses. But I was very pretty," Julie's grandmother said, smoothing her hair.

"You are still very pretty," Julie's grandfather said and he kissed her cheek.

"In Russia your grandmother sewed for royalty. She made stitches so small they couldn't be seen. People wondered how the dresses stayed together."

"That part is true," Julie's grandmother said proudly.

"As soon as I met your grandmother, I wanted to marry her," Julie's grandfather said. "Every night I hired fireflies to fly over her house and spell out 'Rose, my precious flower, I love you every hour.' And Moishe and I sang love songs under her window.

"Finally her father let me marry her. A year later your mother was born. No one had ever seen such a beautiful child. Then Esther, Ruthie, and Bennie were born and they were just as beautiful. I made them tiny jeweled crowns and they rode through the streets in hand-carved golden baby carriages."

"Enough is enough," Julie's grandmother said. "From now on I insist that Julie hear only the truth. Grandpa and I had to work even harder to feed all those babies but we didn't mind. We had something more valuable than jeweled crowns and golden baby carriages. We had each other and we were free to live as we wanted."

"That's the truth, Rose dear," Julie's grandfather said. "And from now on that's all that will pass through my lips."

They sat quietly for a few minutes. Then Julie's grandfather smiled and whispered to Julie, "Did I ever tell you about the time Moishe the goat and I sang for President Wilson?"

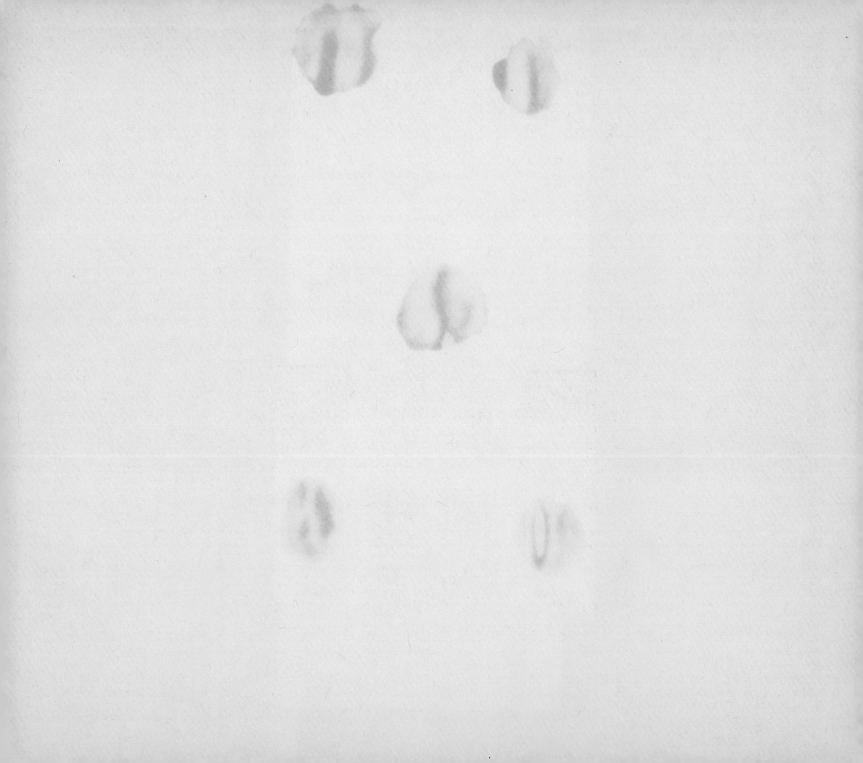

E
HEL Heller, Linda

Copy 2

The casle on Hester

Street